Sara's Potty

Harriet Ziefert · Illustrated by Emily Bolam

Who sits on the potty?
Does a zebra sit on the potty?

Does a sheep sit on the potty?

Does a giraffe sit on the potty?

Does Sara sit on the potty?

What is Sara doing?
She's playing with her potty.

Now what's Sara doing?

Then what does Sara do?

Look at Sara. What is she wearing?